HOW Yussel Caught THE Gefilte Fish

A Shabbos Story

by Charlotte Herman · illustrated by Katya Krenina

DUTTON CHILDREN'S BOOKS · NEW YORK

Library of Congress Cataloging-in-Publication Data

Herman, Charlotte.
How Yussel caught the gefilte fish: a Shabbos story/
by Charlotte Herman; illustrated by Katya Krenina.—1st ed.
p.   cm.
Summary: When he goes fishing with his father for the first time,
a young boy hopes to catch the gefilte fish for his family's Shabbos dinner,
but instead he catches a carp, a trout, and a pike.
ISBN 0-525-45449-7
[1. Jews—United States—Fiction. 2. Sabbath—Fiction. 3. Fishing—Fiction.
4. Family life—Fiction] I. Krenina, Katya, ill. II. Title.
PZ7.H4313Hr   1999   [E]—dc21   97-3792   CIP   AC

Published in the United States 1999 by Dutton Children's Books,
a division of Penguin Putnam Books for Young Readers,
345 Hudson Street, New York, New York 10014
http://www.penguinputnam.com/yreaders/index.htm

Designed by Amy Berniker
Printed in Hong Kong   First Edition
1 3 5 7 9 10 8 6 4 2

For my Uncle Jack,
who catches the best gefilte fish,
and for my Aunt Sue,
who gets hers from a jar

—C.H.

To dearest Flora, Michelle, and Mikhail, with love

—K.K.

Yussel loved gefilte fish. Mama served it every Friday night for their special Shabbos meal. And Yussel loved Shabbos, the day of rest. It began on Friday when the sun went down behind the hills, and it lasted all the next day until three stars appeared in the evening sky.

Mama and Papa did no work on Shabbos. Yussel went with them to visit friends and relatives, and they took long walks through the park.

They ate special foods on Shabbos. And the most special food of all was the gefilte fish. Presented on a platter with parsley and cooked carrots, the large, round balls of fish looked almost as good as they tasted. But even though Mama was the one who served the gefilte fish, it was Papa who caught it.

Every Friday morning, before anyone else woke up, even before the sun was up, Papa slipped out of the house and went fishing in Vasser Lake. Yussel always wanted to go with Papa. He wanted to catch a gefilte fish, too. But Papa always said, "You will have to wait until you are older."

Then early one Friday morning, before Papa slipped out of the house, he came into Yussel's room. "Wake up, Yussel," he whispered. "Wake up."

"What's wrong, Papa?" asked Yussel, rubbing his eyes.

"Nothing is wrong," said Papa. "We are going fishing. You and I are going to catch the gefilte fish for Shabbos."

"Me? I'm going, too?" asked Yussel.

"Yes," said Papa. "Now hurry. Before all the fish are caught, and there won't be any left for us."

Yussel leaped out of bed and dressed quickly. Then he went outside, where Papa was waiting for him with a fishing pole, a basket, and a pail. Papa handed Yussel the fishing pole, and they started their mile-long walk to Vasser Lake.

Yussel had never been up so early. He had never seen the sky so rosy red. All the stores were closed, and no children were playing in the streets. But he was wide awake and going fishing with Papa. And he had a fishing pole.

"I have always loved this time of morning," said Papa. "So still. So quiet. But sometimes I was lonely walking by myself. Now I have you."

"We are the only ones awake in the whole town," said Yussel.

"Yes," said Papa. "You and me and the gefilte fish."

As Yussel and Papa walked together, Yussel thought of all the gefilte fish he would catch. All those fat, round gefilte fish for Shabbos. Wouldn't Mama be surprised!

"Did you go fishing when you were a little boy?" Yussel asked.

"I went with my papa. Just as you are going with me now. Only we went by wagon, with our horse, Pitzeleh, leading the way. We went through fields of wheat and wildflowers. I loved those Fridays with my papa. And after you were born, I dreamed of the day you would be old enough to go fishing with me."

"And now I'm old enough, right?" asked Yussel, skipping alongside
Papa.

"Yes," said Papa. "On Passover, when I saw how you sat through the
whole seder until late at night, how you asked questions and listened to
the answers, I knew you were ready."

As the sky turned pink, they entered a clearing in the woods and came to Vasser Lake. Tall weeds grew out of the water.

"This is the best spot," said Papa, setting the basket and pail on the ground. "Here we will catch lots of fish."

They sat down on the grassy bank. Papa reached into the basket. "First we need the bait. And there is nothing better than your mama's fresh challah dough. Gefilte fish can't resist it."

"Let me, Papa. Let me help put on the bait."

Yussel and Papa attached the dough onto the fishing hook at the end of the line. Papa dropped the line into the water and handed the pole to Yussel. "Time to go fishing," he said.

"How will I know when the fish bites the challah dough?" asked Yussel.

"You will know," Papa answered.

The sky grew lighter. Papa hummed softly—very softly, so as not to frighten away the fish. Yussel hummed along with him.

Suddenly Yussel felt a tug at the end of his line.

"Papa! I think I caught something! I hope it's a gefilte."

"So do I," said Papa.

The fish flipped and flopped. It jumped and splashed.

"It looks like you caught a big one," said Papa. "Hold on tightly."

The fish pulled and tugged for a long time. And when its tugs grew weaker, Yussel, with Papa's help, hauled it in.

It was a big, fat, gold-colored fish with large scales. "It's a beautiful fish," said Papa. "Nice and *zaftig*. It reminds me of your aunt Goldie."

"But it isn't a gefilte fish," said Yussel when he saw that it wasn't round like a ball.

"No," said Papa. "It's a carp. But we'll keep it anyway." He took the hook out and placed the fish inside the pail.

Yussel and Papa washed their hands in Vasser Lake. Then they ate a breakfast of bread and cheese that Mama had packed for them in the basket. "Gefilte fish like cheese, too," said Papa when they were finished. He broke off a piece and gave it to Yussel. "Put it on tight so it won't fall off."

Yussel hooked the cheese and threw his line out. To make sure the cheese held, he dangled the bait above the gentle ripples in the water. Suddenly the water exploded; a fish leaped out, swallowed the cheese, and dove back in.

"Papa!" Yussel cried out.

"Hold on!" shouted Papa. He grabbed onto the pole, and they yanked the fish out of the water. The fish went flying through the air and landed, flipping and flopping on the ground.

"Did you see, Papa? Did you see what just happened?"

"I have never seen anything like it before," said Papa. "This time the fish caught us. Who would believe it?"

The fish had brown spots and tiny scales. It wasn't round like a ball.

"This isn't gefilte fish, either," said Yussel. "Who ever heard of a gefilte fish with brown spots?"

"It's a trout," said Papa. "But we'll keep it anyway." He put the trout in the pail with the carp. "Such a lively fish that was. So eager to please. Just like your cousin Hannah Rose."

For the next fish, Papa showed Yussel how to put a worm on the hook. "Gefilte fish also like worms," he said.

Yussel waited quietly for a fish to bite. The sun was higher in the sky now, and it warmed his shoulders. Suddenly he felt a yank at the end of his line.

"Papa! A fish! I caught another fish! Oh, please let it be a gefilte."
The fish pulled one way, Yussel and Papa pulled the other. The fish
tugged, Yussel and Papa tugged. Yussel felt the pole slipping away. He
was sure the fish would pull it right out of their hands. Even worse,
Yussel and Papa would go with it.

"This one is a fighter," Papa said. The words were hardly out of his
mouth when the fish jumped up and sprayed water all over them.

"Ah, so you want to fight?" said Papa. "We'll give you a fight."

With water dripping down his face, Yussel started laughing. "Look, Papa! We're playing tug-of-war with a fish!"

The battle went on for a long time, and Yussel and Papa were getting tired.

"He is stubborn, this one," said Papa. "He has a mind of his own. Just like Uncle Harry."

Finally the fish gave up its fight, and they hauled it in. It was long and slender and yellow-spotted.

"It isn't a gefilte," said Yussel, sighing. "It's the wrong shape and the wrong color."

"It's a pike," said Papa. "But we'll keep it anyway." He put the pike into the pail with the trout and the carp.

The sun climbed higher. Yussel and Papa were wet and tired.

"Time to go," said Papa.

"Please, not yet," said Yussel. "We didn't catch any gefilte."

"Don't worry," said Papa, putting an arm around Yussel's shoulders.
"Your mama can work miracles."

When they reached their house they could already smell the Shabbos meal cooking: the chicken roasting in the oven and the chicken soup simmering on the stove. Mama smiled when she saw Yussel and Papa.
"Two wet fishermen and three nice fish. How wonderful!"
"A carp, a trout, and a pike," said Papa. "And Yussel caught them all."
"But no gefilte fish for Shabbos," said Yussel.
"Don't worry," said Mama. "Tonight, as always, we will have our gefilte fish."

Yussel watched and waited for Mama to work her miracles. He watched her clean and skin the fish. Then she cut it up and chopped it in her wooden bowl. Mama let Yussel help her add eggs and onions, bread crumbs and sugar, salt and pepper, and mix everything together.

They formed the mixture into balls.
"Gefilte fish!" Yussel cried out when he saw what they had made.
"Not yet," said Mama, dropping them into a pot of boiling water.

After the fish had cooked and the pot had cooled, Mama took out each piece and placed it on a large platter. She surrounded the fish with carrots and parsley.

Yussel recognized the familiar platter. "Gefilte fish!" he cried out again. "We made gefilte fish!"

"Almost," said Mama. "We need just one more seasoning. A special spice."

"What is the special spice?" asked Yussel.
Mama basted the chicken and didn't answer.
"Why is it special?"
Mama stirred the soup.
"When will we add the spice?"
Mama just smiled.

Aunt Goldie and Hannah Rose came early to help Mama with the last-minute preparations. And just before sundown, everything was ready. The house was spotless. The table was set with a white cloth, silver candlesticks, and Mama's best dishes.

Yussel and Papa, dressed in their finest clothes, went to synagogue and came home with Uncle Harry and a Shabbos visitor from another town— a white-bearded tailor named Morris.

"Good Shabbos, good Shabbos, a peaceful Shabbos," they all wished one another.

Everyone sat down at the table. Yussel sat next to Papa. Warmed by the glow of the Shabbos lights, he listened as Papa welcomed the Shabbos with blessings over the wine and challah loaves. Yussel took a sip of the sweet, red wine. He tasted a piece of Mama's soft, fresh challah.

Then it was time to eat. But before the golden chicken soup, before the roast chicken and sweetened carrots, before the Shabbos songs, Mama brought out the platter of fish. There were exclamations of *oohs* and *aahs*. Yussel looked for the special spice but didn't see it.

"Ah, what would Shabbos be without gefilte fish," said the tailor, helping himself to a piece.

"Shabbos without gefilte fish is like a wedding without dancing," said Aunt Goldie, taking two pieces.

"What do you mean?" asked Uncle Harry. "Without gefilte fish, there *is* no Shabbos."

"This is delicious," said Aunt Goldie, licking her lips.

"A *mechaieh*," said Uncle Harry, closing his eyes. "Such a treat."

"The best I have ever tasted," said the tailor.

"You caught wonderful gefilte fish," Hannah Rose told Papa.

"Yussel caught them this time," said Papa.

"Yes," said Yussel, smiling. "I caught the gefilte fish. But Papa helped." And everyone laughed.

Yussel looked around the room. The Shabbos lights cast a glow across the table. They shone on Mama and Papa. They shone on Aunt Goldie and Uncle Harry. They shone on Hannah Rose and the tailor named Morris.

Yussel tasted the fish. It tasted more delicious than ever before.

With his family around him, and their smiling faces shining on him, Yussel felt the Shabbos peace. So that was the special spice! He smiled at Mama and Papa.

Now it was gefilte fish.

Glossary

The following words are Yiddish, a language derived from Hebrew and German:

CHALLAH (KHA-la): a braided bread eaten on the Sabbath (Shabbos) and Jewish festivals

GEFILTE FISH (ge-FILL-teh FISH): ground fish that, mixed with eggs, bread or matzoh crumbs, and seasonings, is shaped into round or oval balls and cooked

MECHAIEH (m'-KHY-eh): pleasure, enjoyment

SHABBOS (SHAH-biss): the Sabbath, day of rest

ZAFTIG (ZOFF-tig): plump

⧸⧹⧸⧹⧸⧹⧸⧹⧸⧹⧸⧹⧸⧹⧸⧹⧸⧹⧸⧹⧸⧹⧸⧹

Gefilte Fish

One of the ways Jewish people show their delight in the Sabbath is by eating fish. Gefilte fish (*gefilte* meaning "stuffed" in Yiddish) became popular with the Jews of Eastern Europe partly because many people couldn't afford to buy large amounts of fish for their Friday night meal. But by adding filler (matzoh meal or bread crumbs, eggs and onions) to ground fish, they were able to make enough fish for everyone in the family to enjoy on the Sabbath.

In the story, Yussel's mama made gefilte fish with a mixture of carp, trout, and pike because those were the fish that Yussel and Papa caught. But you can use almost any kind of fish. Here is one of my favorite (and easy!) recipes using just whitefish:

FOR GEFILTE FISH BALLS:
2 pounds whitefish fillets (ground)
2 medium onions (grated)
2 medium carrots (grated)
2 large eggs
$^1/_2$ cup matzoh meal or bread crumbs
2 teaspoons salt
$^1/_2$ teaspoon pepper
$^1/_4$ cup sugar (optional*)

FOR ADDING TO THE
BOILING WATER:
4 medium carrots (sliced)
2 medium onions (sliced)
a few onion skins (to give
the fish a golden color)
2 teaspoons salt
$^1/_2$ teaspoon pepper
$^1/_4$ cup sugar (optional*)

Place 2 quarts of water in a large pot to boil. In a large bowl, combine the gefilte fish ingredients and mix thoroughly. With wet hands, shape mixture into balls. When the water has boiled, add the carrots and onions and other remaining ingredients, then carefully drop in the fish balls. Cover pot and simmer for $1^1/_2$ hours. Let cool a little, then remove the fish balls and carrots from the pot and chill in the refrigerator. Serve the fish cold, with a garnish of the cooked carrots, some fresh parsley, and red horseradish (I like the sweet kind).
Yields 10 to 12 pieces.

*Some people like sweet gefilte fish, others don't. If you prefer fish that isn't sweet, omit the sugar.

⧸⧹⧸⧹⧸⧹⧸⧹⧸⧹⧸⧹⧸⧹⧸⧹⧸⧹⧸⧹⧸⧹